Beyond the Pale

by

Rudyard Kipling

Rise of Douai

Copyright © 2014 Rise of Douai

All rights reserved.

ISBN-13:
978-1502801708

ISBN-10:
1502801701

Introduction

Joseph Rudyard Kipling (30 December 1865 – 18 January 1936 was an English short-story writer, poet, and novelist. He wrote tales and poems of British soldiers in India and stories for children. He was born in Bombay, in the Bombay Presidency of British India, and was taken by his family to England when he was five years old.

Kipling's works of fiction include The Jungle Book (a collection of stories which includes "Rikki-Tikki-Tavi"), the Just So Stories (1902), Kim (1901), and many short stories, including "The Man Who Would Be King" (1888). His poems include "Mandalay" (1890), "Gunga Din" (1890), "The Gods of the Copybook Headings" (1919), "The White Man's Burden" (1899), and "If—" (1910). He is regarded as a major innovator in the art of the short story; his children's books are enduring classics of children's literature; and one critic described his work as exhibiting "a versatile and luminous narrative gift".

Kipling was one of the most popular writers in England, in both prose and verse, in the late

19th and early 20th centuries. Henry James said: "Kipling strikes me personally as the most complete man of genius (as distinct from fine intelligence) that I have ever known." In 1907, he was awarded the Nobel Prize in Literature, making him the first English-language writer to receive the prize, and its youngest recipient to date. Among other honours, he was sounded out for the British Poet Laureateship and on several occasions for a knighthood, all of which he declined.

Kipling's subsequent reputation has changed according to the political and social climate of the age and the resulting contrasting views about him continued for much of the 20th century. George Orwell called him a "prophet of British imperialism". Literary critic Douglas Kerr wrote: "He [Kipling] is still an author who can inspire passionate disagreement and his place in literary and cultural history is far from settled. But as the age of the European empires recedes, he is recognised as an incomparable, if controversial, interpreter of how empire was experienced. That, and an increasing recognition of his extraordinary narrative gifts, make him a force to be reckoned with.

Beyond the Pale

"Love heeds not caste nor sleep a broken bed. I went in search of
   love and lost myself."

Hindu Proverb.

A man should, whatever happens, keep to his own caste, race and breed. Let the White go to the White and the Black to the Black. Then, whatever trouble falls is in the ordinary course of things— neither sudden, alien, nor unexpected.

This is the story of a man who wilfully stepped beyond the safe limits of decent everyday society, and paid for it heavily.

He knew too much in the first instance; and he saw too much in the second. He took too deep an interest in native life; but he will never do so again.

Deep away in the heart of the City, behind Jitha Megji's bustee, lies Amir Nath's Gully, which ends in a dead-wall pierced by one grated window. At the head of the Gully is a big cow-byre, and the walls on either side of the Gully are without windows. Neither Suchet Singh nor Gaur Chand approved of their women-folk looking into the world. If Durga Charan had been of their opinion, he would have been a happier man to-day, and little Biessa would have been able to knead her own bread. Her room looked out through the grated window into the narrow dark Gully where the sun never came and where the buffaloes wallowed in the blue slime. She was a widow, about fifteen years old, and she prayed the Gods, day and night, to send her a lover; for she did not approve of living alone.

One day the man—Trejago his name was—came into Amir Nath's Gully on an aimless wandering; and, after he had passed the buffaloes, stumbled over a big heap of cattle food.

Then he saw that the Gully ended in a trap, and heard a little laugh from behind the grated window. It was a pretty little laugh, and Trejago, knowing that, for all practical purposes, the old Arabian Nights are good guides, went forward to the window, and whispered that verse of "The Love Song of Har Dyal" which begins:

Can a man stand upright in the face of the naked Sun;
    or a Lover in the Presence of his Beloved?
If my feet fail me, O Heart of my Heart, am I to blame,
    being blinded by the glimpse of your beauty?

There came the faint tchinks of a woman's bracelets from behind the grating, and a little voice went on with the song at the fifth verse:

Alas! alas! Can the Moon tell the Lotus of her love when the
    Gate of Heaven is shut and the clouds gather for the rains?
They have taken my Beloved, and driven her with the pack-horses
    to the North.
There are iron chains on the feet that were set on my heart.

Call to the bowman to make ready—

The voice stopped suddenly, and Trejago walked out of Amir Nath's Gully, wondering who in the world could have capped "The Love Song of Har Dyal" so neatly.

Next morning, as he was driving to the office, an old woman threw a packet into his dog-cart. In the packet was the half of a broken glass bangle, one flower of the blood red dhak, a pinch of bhusa or cattle-food, and eleven cardamoms. That packet was a letter—not a clumsy compromising letter, but an innocent, unintelligible lover's epistle.

Trejago knew far too much about these things, as I have said. No Englishman should be able to translate object-letters. But Trejago spread all the trifles on the lid of his office-box and began to puzzle them out.

A broken glass-bangle stands for a Hindu widow all India over; because, when her husband dies a woman's bracelets are broken on her wrists. Trejago saw the meaning of the little bit of the glass. The flower of the dhak means diversely "desire," "come," "write," or "danger," according to the other things with it. One cardamom means "jealousy;" but when any article is duplicated in an object-letter, it loses its symbolic meaning and stands merely for one of a number indicating time, or, if incense, curds, or saffron be sent also, place. The message ran then:—"A widow—dhak flower and bhusa—at eleven o'clock." The pinch of bhusa enlightened Trejago. He saw— this kind of letter leaves much to instinctive knowledge—that the bhusa referred to the big heap of cattle-food over which he had fallen in Amir Nath's Gully, and that the message must come from the person behind the grating; she being a widow. So the message ran then:—"A widow, in the Gully in which is the heap of bhusa, desires you to come at eleven o'clock."

Trejago threw all the rubbish into the fireplace and laughed. He knew that men in the East do not make love under windows at eleven in the forenoon, nor do women fix appointments a week in advance. So he went, that very night at eleven, into Amir Nath's Gully, clad in a boorka, which cloaks a man as well as a woman. Directly the gongs in the City made the hour, the little voice behind the grating took up "The Love Song of Har Dyal" at the verse where the Panthan girl calls upon Har Dyal to return. The song is really pretty in the Vernacular. In English you miss the wail of it. It runs something like this:—

> Alone upon the housetops, to the North
>   I turn and watch the lightning in the sky,—
>   The glamour of thy footsteps in the North,
>   Come back to me, Beloved, or I die!
>
> Below my feet the still bazar is laid
>   Far, far below the weary camels lie,—
>   The camels and the captives of thy raid,
>   Come back to me, Beloved, or I die!
>
> My father's wife is old and harsh with years,
>   And drudge of all my father's house am I.—
>   My bread is sorrow and my drink is tears,
>   Come back to me, Beloved, or I die!

As the song stopped, Trejago stepped up under the grating and whispered:—"I am here."

Bisesa was good to look upon.

That night was the beginning of many strange things, and of a double life so wild that Trejago to-day sometimes wonders if it were not all a dream. Bisesa or her old handmaiden who had thrown the object-letter had detached the heavy grating from the brick-work of the wall; so that the window slid inside, leaving only a square of raw masonry, into which an active man might climb.

In the day-time, Trejago drove through his routine of office-work, or put on his calling-clothes and called on the ladies of the Station; wondering how long they would know him if they knew of poor little Bisesa. At night, when all the City was still, came the walk under the evil-smelling boorka, the patrol through Jitha Megji's bustee, the quick turn into Amir Nath's Gully between the sleeping cattle and the dead walls, and then, last of all, Bisesa, and the deep, even breathing of the old woman who slept outside the door of the bare little room that Durga Charan allotted to his sister's daughter. Who or what Durga Charan was, Trejago never inquired; and why in the world he was not discovered and knifed never occurred to him till his madness was over, and Bisesa . . . But this comes later.

Bisesa was an endless delight to Trejago. She was as ignorant as a bird; and her distorted versions of the rumors from the outside world that had reached her in her room, amused Trejago almost as much as her lisping attempts to pronounce his name—"Christopher." The first syllable was always more than she could manage, and she made funny little gestures with her rose-leaf hands, as one throwing the name away, and then, kneeling before Trejago, asked him, exactly as an Englishwoman would do, if he were sure he loved her. Trejago swore that he loved her more than any one else in the world. Which was true.

After a month of this folly, the exigencies of his other life compelled Trejago to be especially attentive to a lady of his acquaintance. You may take it for a fact that anything of this kind is not only noticed and discussed by a man's own race, but by some hundred and fifty natives as well. Trejago had to walk with this lady and talk to her at the Band-stand, and once or twice to drive with her; never for an instant dreaming that this would affect his dearer out-of-the-way life. But the news flew, in the usual mysterious fashion, from mouth to mouth, till Bisesa's duenna heard of it and told Bisesa. The child was so troubled that she did the household work evilly, and was beaten by Durga Charan's wife in consequence.

A week later, Bisesa taxed Trejago with the flirtation. She understood no gradations and spoke openly. Trejago laughed and Bisesa stamped her little feet—little feet, light as marigold flowers, that could lie in the palm of a man's one hand.

Much that is written about "Oriental passion and impulsiveness" is exaggerated and compiled at second-hand, but a little of it is true; and when an Englishman finds that little, it is quite as startling as any passion in his own proper life. Bisesa raged and stormed, and finally threatened to kill herself if Trejago did not at once drop the alien Memsahib who had come between them. Trejago tried to explain, and to show her that she did not understand these things from a Western standpoint. Bisesa drew herself up, and said simply:

"I do not. I know only this—it is not good that I should have made you dearer than my own heart to me, Sahib. You are an Englishman. I am only a black girl"—she was fairer than bar-gold in the Mint— "and the widow of a black man."

Then she sobbed and said: "But on my soul and my Mother's soul, I love you. There shall no harm come to you, whatever happens to me."

Trejago argued with the child, and tried to soothe her, but she seemed quite unreasonably disturbed. Nothing would satisfy her save that all relations between them should end. He was to go away at once. And he went. As he dropped out at the window, she kissed his forehead twice, and he walked away wondering.

A week, and then three weeks, passed without a sign from Bisesa. Trejago, thinking that the rupture had lasted quite long enough, went down to Amir Nath's Gully for the fifth time in the three weeks, hoping that his rap at the sill of the shifting grating would be answered. He was not disappointed.

There was a young moon, and one stream of light fell down into Amir Nath's Gully, and struck the grating, which was drawn away as he knocked. From the black dark, Bisesa held out her arms into the moonlight. Both hands had been cut off at the wrists, and the stumps were nearly healed.

Then, as Bisesa bowed her head between her arms and sobbed, some one in the room grunted like a wild beast, and something sharp—knife, sword or spear—thrust at Trejago in his boorka. The stroke missed his body, but cut into one of the muscles of the groin, and he limped slightly from the wound for the rest of his days.

The grating went into its place. There was no sign whatever from inside the house—

nothing but the moonlight strip on the high wall, and the blackness of Amir Nath's Gully behind.

The next thing Trejago remembers, after raging and shouting like a madman between those pitiless walls, is that he found himself near the river as the dawn was breaking, threw away his boorka and went home bareheaded.

What the tragedy was—whether Bisesa had, in a fit of causeless despair, told everything, or the intrigue had been discovered and she tortured to tell, whether Durga Charan knew his name, and what became of Bisesa—Trejago does not know to this day. Something horrible had happened, and the thought of what it must have been comes upon Trejago in the night now and again, and keeps him company till the morning. One special feature of the case is that he does not know where lies the front of Durga Charan's house. It may open on to a courtyard common to two or more houses, or it may lie behind any one of the gates of Jitha Megji's bustee. Trejago cannot tell. He cannot get Bisesa—poor little Bisesa—back again. He has lost her in the City, where each man's house is as guarded and as unknowable as the grave; and the grating that opens into Amir Nath's Gully has been walled up.

But Trejago pays his calls regularly, and is reckoned a very decent sort of man.

There is nothing peculiar about him, except a slight stiffness, caused by a riding-strain, in the right leg.

THE END

RISE OF DOUAI

RISE OF DOUAI

TWITTER : @RISEOFDOUAI

© 2013, PUBLISHED BY RISE OF DOUAI PUBLISHING, OTHER PUBLICATIONS:

- AN IDIOT'S GUIDE TO: BEE HUNTING BY JOHN LOCKARD, EDITED BY ARSALAN AHMED (2012)(PAPERBACK) ISBN-10: 1478383550

- THE RISE OF DOUAI BY ARSALAN AHMED (2012)(PAPERBACK) ISBN-10: 1479267783

- THE RICHEST MAN IN BABYLON BY GEORGE S. CLASON (2012) (PAPERBACK) ISBN-10: 1479377341

- THINK AND GROW RICH BY NAPOLEON HILL (2012) (PAPERBACK) ISBN-10: 1480061638

- AS A MAN THINKETH BY MR JAMES ALLEN (2012) (PAPERBACK) ISBN-10: 1480088161
- HOW TO ANALYZE PEOPLE ON

SIGHT BY ELSIE BENEDICT (PAPERBACK) ISBN-10: 1480081272
- THE ART OF WAR BY MR SUN TZU (PAPERBACK) ISBN-10: 1480082007
- MACBETH BY MR WILLIAM SHAKESPEARE (PAPERBACK) ISBN-10: 1480060682
- A CHRISTMAS CAROL BY MR CHARLES DICKENS ISBN-10: 1481194755
- CREATING CAPITAL: MONEY-MAKING AS AN AIM IN BUSINESS BY MR FREDRICK L LIPMAN ISBN-10: 1481158996
- GETTING GOLD: A PRACTICAL TREATISE FOR PROSPECTORS, MINERS, AND STUDENTS BY MR JOSEPH COLIN FRANCIS JOHNSON ISBN-10: 1481090984
- THE INTERPRETATION OF DREAMS BY MR SIGMUND FREUD ISBN-10: 1481134558
- THE COMMUNIST MANIFESTO BY MR KARL MARX AND MR FRIDRICK ENGLES ISBN-10:

1480112445
- THE PRINCE BY MR NICCOLO MACHIAVELLI ISBN-10: 1480119601
- THE WAY TO WEALTH BY MR BENJAMIN FRANKLIN ISBN-10: 1480099651

- THE ART OF MONEY GETTING - OR GOLDEN RULES FOR MAKING MONEY (SUCCESS PRINCIPLES) BY MR PHINEAS TAYLOR BARNUM ISBN-10: 1480138622

Twitter : **@RiseofDouai**

Printed in Great Britain
by Amazon